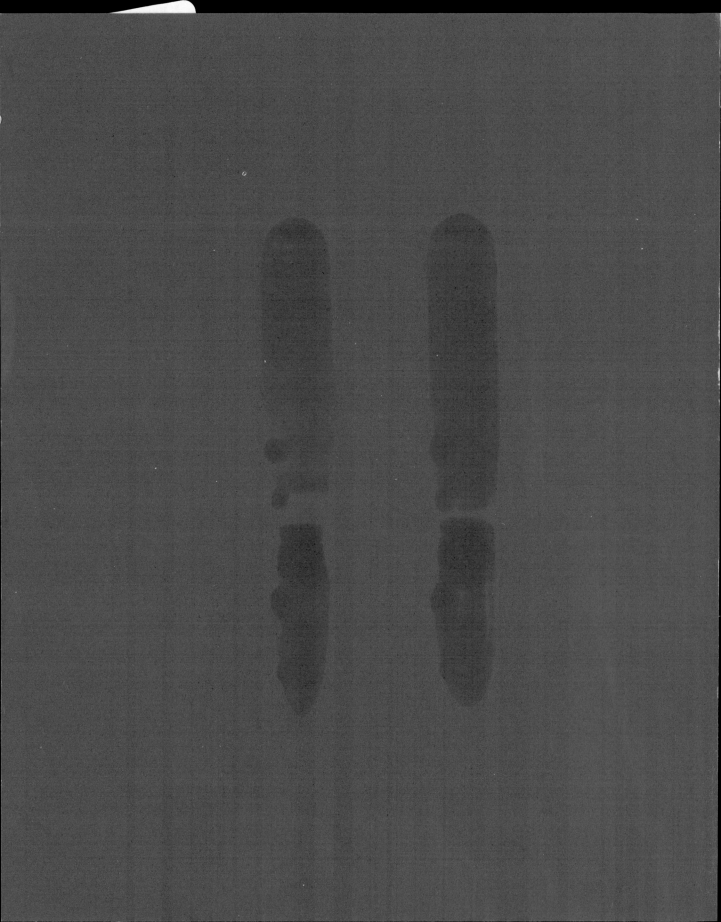

Goblin Walk

Goblin Walk

Tony Johnston · Bruce Degen

G. P. Putnam's Sons   New York

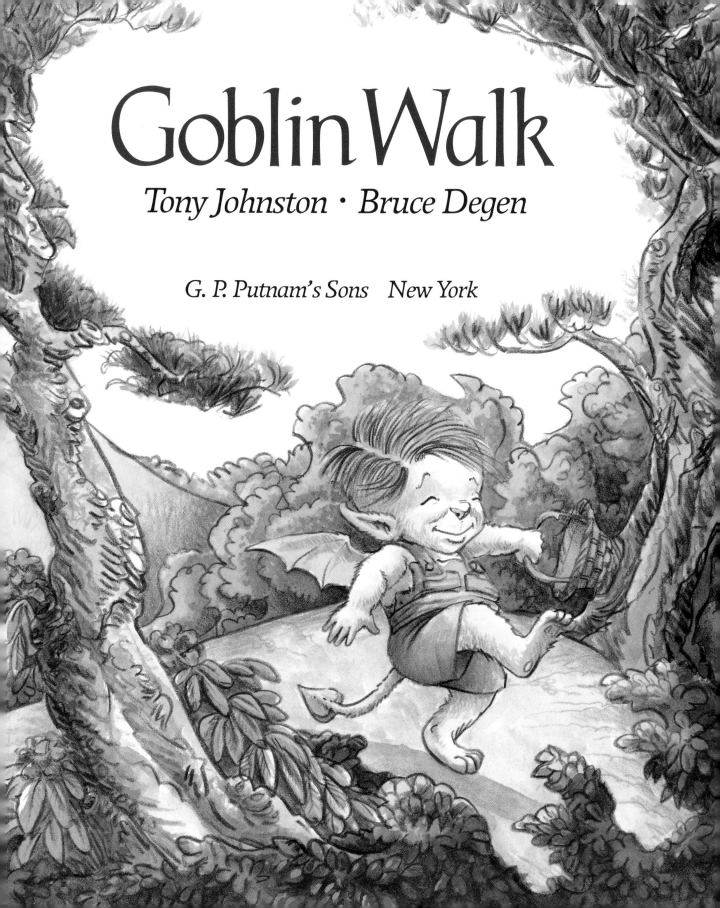

Library of Congress Cataloging-in-Publication Data
Johnston, Tony.
Goblin walk / by Tony Johnston : illustrated by Bruce Degen.
p. cm.
Summary: A little goblin has a series of frightening experiences
while walking through the woods to his grandmother's house.
ISBN 0-399-22238-3
[1. Goblins—Fiction. 2. Fear—Fiction. 3. Humorous stories.]
I. Degen, Bruce, ill. II. Title.
PZ7.J6478Go 1991 [E]—dc20 90-22985 CIP AC

10 9 8 7 6 5 4 3 2 1
FIRST IMPRESSION

For Lauren and Greeny.
Who else?
—T.J.

For Fran Manushkin,
who got me started.
—B.D.

little goblin
was walking through a wood,
taking some rocks to his grandmother.
Now and then he hopped in the air.
And he gnashed his teeth,
he felt so good. BUT—

he rounded a bend, and what did he see?

A mouse!

"Oh-oh-oh!" cried the goblin.
For he was as scared as can be.

"No-no-no!" squeaked the mouse.
And it ran away, one, two, three.

The little goblin kept walking through the wood,
taking weeds to his grandmother, too.
Now and then he danced in the air.
And he growled out loud, he felt so good. BUT—
he rounded a bend, and what did he see?

A squirrel!
"Yelp-yelp-yelp!" yowled the goblin.
For he was as scared as can be.
"Help-help-help!" howled the squirrel.
And it ran away, one, two, three.

The little goblin kept walking through the wood,
taking bugs to his grandmother, too.
Now and then he pranced in the air.
And he snarled for joy,
he felt so good. BUT—
he rounded a bend, and what did he see?

A bird!
"Hi-hi-hi!" screamed the goblin.
For he was as scared as can be.
"Yi-yi-yi!" screeched the bird.
And it flew away, one, two, three.

The little goblin kept walking through the wood,
taking thorns to his grandmother, too.
Now and then he jumped in the air.
And he stuck out his tongue at a tree. BUT—
he rounded a bend, and what did he see?

A butterfly!
"Yee-yee-yee!" squeaked the goblin.
For he was as scared as can be.
"Eee-eee-eee!" thought the butterfly
(for it could not talk). And it flew away, one, two, three.

The little goblin kept walking through the wood,
taking peppercorns to his grandmother, too.
Now and then he clicked his heels in the air.
And he made faces at the sun, just for fun. BUT—
he rounded a bend, and what did he see?

A bunny!
He was so horribly scared of that bunny,
he shrieked, "Jeeby-jeeby-jeeby!"
And he ran all the rest of the way.

"Greeny!" he cried.
And he rushed into his grandmother's furry, furry arms.
"Whatever is it?" asked Greeny, hugging him tight.
"I had a great fright!"

"Tell me all," said she. SO—
he did.
"I saw bad things in the wood. I saw a mouse."
"That is bad," said Greeny.
"I saw a squirrel."
"That is bad," said Greeny.
"I saw a bird and a butterfly and a *bunny*!"
"Bad, bad, BAD," Greeny said.
"But never fear. I am here. And that is good."

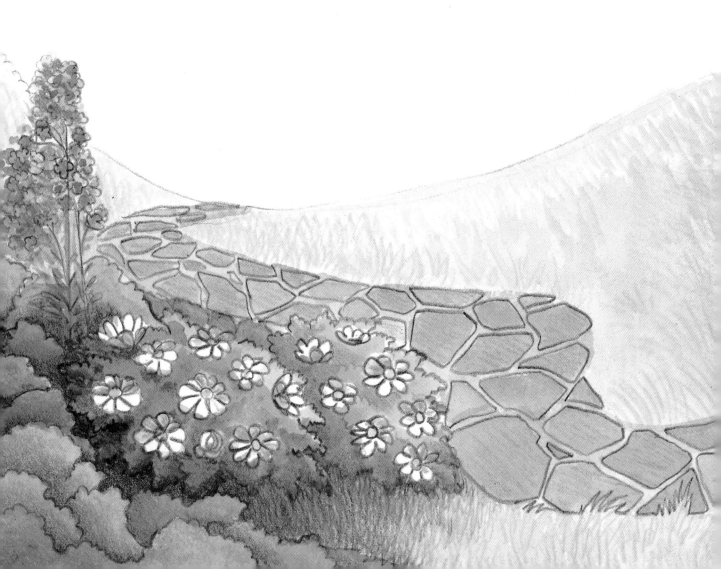

Then the little goblin cried, "Tee-hee-hee!"
For he remembered something else good.
What was it?
His presents.

"Greeny," he said, "I brought you good things.
I brought rocks."
"That is good," Greeny said.
"I brought weeds."
"That is good," Greeny said.
"I brought bugs and thorns and peppercorns."

"Good, good, GOOD," said she.
"I'll make cookies for you and me." SO—
she did.
The little goblin helped.

And they gobbled some, one, two, three.
Then it was time to go home.

Greeny said, "I will walk with you.
And you will not feel scared." SO—
A little goblin was walking through a wood,
taking some cookies to his mother.
Now and then he skipped in the air.
And the whole wood jiggled.
And he giggled, he felt so good.

And guess what?
All the way home they never saw a thing.
Not even a bunny.
Isn't that funny?